A Deadly Game

A Novel

By Benjamin H. Liles

Liles Publishing

A DEADLY GAME

Copyright © 2018 by Benjamin H. Liles
All rights reserved. No part of this publication may be reproduced, stored in a retrieval system, or transmitted in any form or by any means—electronic, mechanical, photocopy, recording, or any other—except for brief quotations in printed reviews, without the prior permission of the publisher.

Interior design by Benjamin H. Liles

Library of Congress Cataloging-in-Publication Data

Liles, Benjamin H.
A Deadly Game / Benjamin H. Liles
p. cm.

ISBN-13: 978-1-72189-472-7
ISBN-10: 1-72189-472-1
1. Crime—fiction.
2. Suspense-fiction.
3. Action—fiction.
I. Title

Published in 2018
Printed in the United States of America

A Deadly Game

Benjamin H. Liles

ONE

Geese flew in a small, tight overhead formation. It's the kind of how a team of fighter jets fly. Not low as they sometimes do, but high above, as if avoiding something hidden.

Carlisle lay on his back, staring up watching the flock fly by. Lying there in the high grass of the field alone, he pondered the meaning of life and what it meant to live it when he felt a kick in his right side.

"Hey," Beau yelled as he tripped.

"Sorry about that."

Beau was a shortened version of Beauregard, and it wasn't like he'd tell anyone of his full name either. He never had in his thirty-one years and wasn't about to start. And at this stage in his life Beau fit much better than his longer name. He was a handsome man, only a few inches shorter than Carlisle stood. Not that Carlisle cared much, but Beau's tanned features swam into Carlisle's view as he stood up. Beau gathered himself as well and looked into the taller man's face.

"Why are you laying in the field, you nitwit!?"

"You sure could hurt a guy's feelings, Beau, with that kind of talk."

"Well, you shouldn't be just laying there in the tall grass." He swore.

"And maybe you shouldn't just watch where you're stepping but also that mouth of yours as well."

Blood appeared on the right side of Carlisle's body, just under his ribcage, where Beau's boot ripped into the shirt as well as flesh.

"Aw, dang, man, I never…"

"It's no worries. It's not like I don't have other shirts to change into."

"Ah-right, I reckon. You shouldn't be out in a field without some kind of warning."

"All right, Beau. I got it."

They both stood in the field, which adjoined their neighborhood, surveying the land and its outcroppings. After a while, both men grew tired of staring into the distance and started marching towards their homes. A dove suddenly showed itself, which Beau took a deft shot at with his gun. Both men stood, remarking at how loud the gun seemed. A smell of honey wafted in on the hot, summer air marking the time close to supper.

"Smells like a Barbecue kind of night, I suppose."

"Beau, you're the only man I know with the sharpest sense of smell, ever. I imagine you're right though, barbecue sounds just right."

"Should I take offense?"

"Take it as you want it, just letting you know you have one sharp sense of smell."

While striding onward towards their homes they both tripped over what they thought was a log.

"Oomph!"

"Dagonne it!"

Both men rolled over to see what tripped them. They looked realized it was the body of Jakes, with a pool of blood surrounding his head. Within what seemed like just minutes, Paul, also known as officer Davison,

A Deadly Game

sidled up to the two men. He was a tall man, six foot two inches, having blue eyes and red hair as well as a red moustache. Along with his looks his demeanor made him seem imposing, if not just by his sheer size.

"Okay, so Beau, where were you before you both found the body of Jakes lying here?"

"We were both further out in the field, watching the country side minding our own business. I shot a dove which flew into my view." He pointed in the direction from which they came.

"Carlisle?"

"It's true enough, officer."

"Anything more to add?"

"I can tell you I was out here minding my own business before Beau tripped over me while I watched geese fly overhead."

"Can anyone vouch for you, Carlisle?" Paul wrote notes on his pad, making the hat on his head flounder like a fish.

"My sister-in-law, Amy, can. She knew exactly when I left to come out here and just ruminate on things."

"And you never heard a sound either?"

"Exactly." However, Beau's gun sounded like it had twice the power on it. Not sure of relevance though. Also, Jakes wasn't anywhere near here when I came this way earlier."

A pack of dogs sounded their call somewhere in the neighborhood, barking at either something they saw or probably just heard. The sound stopped abruptly due to owners of the dogs coming out and shushing them.

Paul simply scratched his head after taking in the sound. "I can tell both of you gentlemen this much, if I need any more from either of you, I'll ask."

"Yes, sir, Sheriff, sir."

Paul rolled his eyes. "Knock it off, Beau!"

"Ah-right, officer."

"That's more like it."

Carlisle stood there a moment, arms crossed over his chest. He mulled over everything. From the geese that flew overhead earlier, to his dearly departed wife; from Beau kicking him accidentally to the body of Jakes lying at the opening of the field. The fact of the matter was he had been in the field not just contemplating why his wife died while geese flew overhead, but silently praying as to why she had to die in the first place. It was why he retired as a police officer himself.

He was more than acquainted with Paul Davison, but had been his partner for almost a decade.

"Hey, Paul?"

"What is it?" Paul stood, looking perturbed over finding Jakes dead as well as where things could lead.

"You do know, if you ever need me, just ask from one old partner to another."

Now he scratched his side. "If I do, I'll let you know, but Carlisle, you know this is an official matter for the law and not for civilians."

"I'm just asking to remain informed."

To Paul it seemed the day just got started and was never going to end. And to Carlisle he wondered how the day could go sideways when it had been such a beautiful, almost cloudless day with geese flying, making their way north?

A Deadly Game

I sat there, half in the shadows of the day, spying as the three men split apart and go their own ways. Sweat beaded up on my forehead and I felt partially guilty for duping the three of them. Sure I killed Jakes at the same moment Beau shot the dove, but that was going to work in my favor; at some point. Beau seemed like a country hick, so he was never going to be a problem to me, if at all. In the same breath though, he could easily be a problem. Things would be so simpler with Beau gone. No one paid him a lot of attention anyway. My plans would be made clearer as things kept going, as I needed them to. Officer Paul Davison wasn't a man cut out to be in law enforcement. He may be a good man, just not swift in the law as I am though.

And as for Carlisle, he seemed as far better an adversary to me. His wife was the icing on the cake the day as I aimed for him. Cat and mouse never looked to be as good a game to me as it had before.

Carlisle noticed the vehicle first. While he was inches taller than
Beau, Paul should have seen it before
he left their wooded subdivision of
Lockhaven. Lockhaven is situated barely five minutes north and ten minutes west of Marble Falls, TX. It had all the beauty of the Texas Hill Country as did the surrounding areas. You could hunt dove, deer (bucks mostly and in season), go fishing either on the three lakes close by.

Inks Lake was primarily a lake with small bass and catfish, where Burnet Lake and Lake LBJ were more along the lines of catfish and carp. Lockhaven also was clearly closer to shopping in terms to Marble

Falls than Burnet was. It took fifteen minutes along the highway to get from Marble Falls to Burnet, but Lockhaven was closer if you took a few back roads. He went inside his home, which he shared with his sister-in-law who cared for him, picked up his sidearm, which he had a permit for, and a flashlight then slipping back out to investigate the vehicle.

It appeared to simply be a rusting pile of metal; a dying burnt out relic someone had placed there to either be an ambush or a good hiding place for kids (as long as they didn't get inside it). As he peered into its frame, where it seemed attached to the road for quite some time, he shone the light.

Whatever Carlisle had to do, he would do it as much a ready man would attack a bear, swift and deadly. He shut off the light that he had and put his gun into its holster on his side. Juan Alvarez, a Hispanic national, working on becoming a United States citizen, walked briskly over to his neighbor and friend. He was a quiet man, somber actually, and with his dark hair and deep brown eyes remained silent a moment.

"What's going on, Juan?"

"Jakes no bad." While his English wasn't all that well fewer people couldn't understand his broken English.

"Come again, Juan?"

"I try again." He thought momentarily, allowing his forehead to crinkle and then looked relieved as if having a revelation. "Jakes did no wrong."

"You're right there, compadre. He did nothing wrong to anyone."

While Alvarez wasn't in the States illegally he also had to work hard in both classes he took as well as the job he held as a security officer for a bank. You could tell Juan was a good guy with a good heart and work ethic. He originally came to the States, before marrying Maria, on a work visa and they happened to fall in love. It was because of her he worked hard on learning the language.

"Listen Juan."

"Si? I mean, yes, Carlisle?"

"You know in a few months we have those elections for Sheriff and all."

Juan just stood staring at Carlisle. "Yes."

"Considering I'm running for the position, mind if I let you in on a secret?"

"¿qué significa secreto? I mean, what is secret?"

"Before I tell you, we may need your wife out here. Mind getting her?"

"¿Mi esposa? Yes, I go get."

Juan's wife, Maria, was a good-looking half-American, half Hispanic woman who stood at five feet four inches. She was as jovial as her husband was and yet spoke English far better than he. She noticed the men down the street and came to Juan as he neared her and brought her back to Carlisle. Even in the dark Carlisle could see her green eyes. They were like cat's eyes in that they could see well in the dark and any light coming in from anywhere cast a glow from her eyes.

"Hello Carlisle."

"Evening, Maria. I need a bit of your help translating between Juan and I."

"No problem, I'm just glad to help. Can you tell me what happened earlier?"

"You know Jakes, right?"

Juan moved next to his wife and she accepted him by putting her arm, as best as she could, around him. "I did, a little."

"Someone shot him."

"Who would do such a thing? He was a sweet man, even if he was a pushover."

"No idea as of yet. Anyway, I was trying to ask Juan if he'd like to be a police officer's deputy; heriff's deputy."

Juan looked like a cat backed into a corner. "¿Policia? Oh, no, no policia!"

She calmly and softly spoke to him, bringing him out of his stupor and explained in Spanish what it was Carlisle needed of him.

"Ah, yes! I can do job!" Now he smiled hugely.

"Well, alright, folks. I better get on in. Juan we'll talk soon. Maria, have a safe and lovely night, ma'am."

Carlisle tipped his hat towards them and sauntered on into his home.

As he walked inside, Maria replied, "Thanks. I'll make sure he knows more English so you can talk without an interpreter." She spoke with a Hispanic lilt, but as she knew English far better, it was just slight if not noticeable.

I sat in the darkness, between houses, watching the exchange between Juan, Carlisle and Maria Alvarez. this might be a bump in my little plans to take care of the business I intended. Rather, I still had to take my time. If I did things too soon or too slow nothing would ever be accomplished. I was going to have to plan things out clearly, carefully and craftily. I walked away from between the houses and went back to mine. Closing the door I made sure no one knew anything of what was to take place next.

TWO

That night he dreamt of his late wife Eliza. Eliza Moore, he realized, was a true and active beauty. She had fair hair and hazel-green eyes, once upon a time. They met when Carlisle Donovan saved up the money for a trip to North Carolina. The day had been warm and not only was she walking up the beach towards him, but he also had been walking the beach as well. She noticed the tousled brown haired man with brown-hazel eyes and sharp, angular nose and thought he looked handsome.

He thought she was some sort of model. He would find out later she was an actress from the United Kingdom. Theirs was a whirlwind kind of romance. It was a bit like a fairy tale. He could ill afford the trips she could make, but then she had the money to do so. He did not. He was just a small town guy, with small town values and that's the life he picked out for himself.

After courting her for around two years and then getting married it was a surprise to him she moved to Lockhaven with him. And when he wasn't working as an officer of the law they had their vacations. It was on one of those vacations that they ran into trouble. As a result he was also called on to help with the investigation.

A man simply known as Raven, with jet-black hair and beady, dark eyes killed two overseas officers. Interpol knew of both men, but for different reasons. They knew of Carlisle's reputation as a peace officer and Raven for his assassin-like qualities. It was for this reason the two men squared off and more than once.

"You must be Carlisle." Raven snarled.

"I am."

"You must be wondering why an international policing organization has you after me."

"That's simple. You're an assassin for hire."

It seemed the two men danced around each other. Raven had a knife drawn and Carlisle waited for him to pounce to make his move. Raven's laugh was like that of a raven; startling. "I will not be underestimated."

"You think that highly of yourself then."

Raven lunged at Carlisle only to find himself pinned against a wall. He felt handcuffs being snapped into place on his wrists and still managed to get away by twisting himself up and around Carlisle.

"Next time, Carl," he yelled into the night.

"Next time, indeed," Carlisle said to himself. It had been the one and only time any one called him that and it was going to be the last time.

He struggled awake, sweating great drops. His sister-in-law, Amy, practically broke into his room checking on him.

"I'm alright, Amy."

"Are you sure? You're breathing heavily."

Amy Moore stood there with a towel ready for him, but looked almost exactly like her sister, just only a few years younger than her.

"I'll be fine, I was just dreaming of the few days Eliza and I had in Cambodia."

A Deadly Game

Amy looked rattled at the news.

"Are you sure you don't need me?" She leaned back over dabbing at spots of sweat off his temple.

"Amy, I give you my word, I'm okay. It was just a bad dream. One that hopefully I'll forget."

She started to walk out of the room, but looked at her brother-in-law and saw why her sister fell for him. When Carlisle said he was fine, he was indeed fine. "Good night, Carlisle."

"Amy?"

She walked back to him a moment. "Yes?"

"Someday, somehow, I will get the man who killed Eliza."

Amy's eyes filled with tears and she closed the door.

After a few more hours of undisturbed sleep, Carlisle woke up, gathering himself and eating breakfast with Amy then headed out the door to attend to his daily business. When he wasn't on the Lockhaven police force, his business was supplying meat to the public.

Abel Ruiz, Carlisle's business manager, helped in the daily running of things so that Carlisle could tend to other matters. Abel was a short yet stocky man with light brown hair and amber-colored eyes.

"Carlisle, we may have to order more wrapping paper."

"I did that last night, Abel."

"Oh? I thought I ran things."

Carlisle ran his hands through his hair.

"It is your business, I just thought I managed."

Carlisle looked up at his friend and manager of his meat packing business. "You are, Abel. I usually look over things making sure we're good on what we need day-to-day. You know that."

Abel appeared to take the answer and brought himself back into good spirits.

A gunshot was heard, glass broke and spidered out with the bullet striking Abel in the chest. Carlisle ran over to him and eased him down.

"You'll be okay, buddy. Just catch your breath."

Carlisle, on the other hand, looked across the street to the tops of the buildings, trying his best to find whoever fired the shot. He looked back down to Abel, noticing his friend was breathing and fairing well.

"Will I be all right?"

"I believe so. We'll find who did this, Abel. I promise that." Carlisle applied pressure to where the shot entered Abel, with a towel he found minutes before and got the bleeding to slow down. "Can you sit up?"

"Let me check." Abel, slowly and painfully sat up, grimacing as he did.

"Boss, I think whoever did this was a little sloppy."

"No. The guy is never sloppy. If he wanted you dead, you wouldn't be talking right now. I'll catch up with you in a while."

By the time Carlisle was on the phone with 9-1-1, people milled about wondering what happened. Within minutes emergency crews loaded Abel up on a stretcher, carting him off to Baylor Scott and White just a little south of Marble Falls.

Juan's wife, Maria, was the first to ask. "Will Abel be alright?"

"He'll be just fine. It's just a flesh wound. Whoever shot him wanted me to respond: which I did. That person will be sorry."

A Deadly Game

"Remember, Carlisle, vengeance belongs to God."

"Thanks, Maria. I'll be fine."

He ended up closing business early. It wasn't like Carlisle's Meat was going to hurt for business and within days they'd be back running as efficiently as ever.

"Do you need help while Abel is getting well?"

"Are you offering?" He searched her face. It wasn't like Juan couldn't cook and feed their children. After all, almost everyone in the Lockhaven area cooked on a nightly basis. If it wasn't one spouse who did, the other would. It just came down to what one wanted for dinner.

"Yes. I am."

"Maria, I have to be honest here. While I know you can do the job, I'm not sure it would be wise."

"You know we need the money, plus until Abel is better you need a manager. I am able to do the job."

Carlisle relented.

From Raven's perch atop Grand Hotel right across from Carlisle's Meat, he chuckled softly to himself. He seemed a bit terrified when Carlisle looked his way just shortly after Abel was shot, but that was a price to pay for wanting the man to be on edge. "He will be a hard man to nail. It will just take time."

That night while at his home Carlisle recounted the day to Amy.

"Abel's got a strong heart on him?" She looked at him while serving him his nightly hot tea.

"Well, rumor has it he outlasted in Vietnam. Your guess is as good as mine on that."

The light danced in her eyes.

"Carlisle, how many years since my sister's passing have we been together?"

Just the thought of Eliza pulled him downward. "Amy, until I catch the man who killed her I can't think of settling back down. You know she was the love of my life."

Amy got down to his level, looked into his eyes and waited until he looked into hers. "You know I love you, right?"

He felt uneasy staring into her eyes as they reminded him so much of Eliza. He shook off the feelings he had for her. "Amy…"

While neither of them made a move, there was an unspoken bond between the two of them. Sooner or later Carlisle would have to face down the feelings they shared to one another.

"At any rate, what do you want for supper?"

"Chili sounds mighty fine, Amy." He came up behind her and held her in his arms momentarily.

"Don't, Carlisle." She turned and pushed him away. "You tell me you can't do anything and yet you hold me that way. Don't mess with my heart that way."

He felt a little deflated but honored her. While he couldn't any time soon be with any other woman, anyone could see that he truly loved Amy as he did Eliza. The chemistry was indeed there.

After dinner had been eaten and Carlisle had washed the dishes, Amy and he sat watching television. Not too very close together, but close enough to have a conversation. It was almost like they were strangers in the same house.

"I'm thinking of going home to Kent for a visit." She furrowed her brow and then moved a strand of her hair back into place.

"Any reason?" He stared with astonishment.

A Deadly Game

"I Just miss my parents is all. They aren't truly the same after Eliza left us." She caught his look.

"Give them my best when and if you decide to go." He stood and walked to the window, peering out at the night sky.

She watched the man she grew to love and realized he was still hurting, but at the same time was enamored with her. "It's not like I won't return. I think we just need a little space. We're too comfortable with each other."

While the two of them never once acted out of passion or otherwise, there was a sense of mutual respect between the two of them.

"So that's what it comes down to." He hung his head, suddenly ashamed for holding her earlier before dinner.

"Carlisle, it's just so we can both think things through."

"I blame myself, you know." He turned to face her. "If it wasn't for the fact that I want the man who killed Eliza behind bars we'd be in a better place."

She stood and stared hard at Carlisle for a moment and then briskly walked from the room, tears streaming down her face. *I am such a fool*, she thought.

The next morning, the sun arose lighting up the sky in radiant colors, signifying the night departed and wouldn't return for another sixteen or so hours. Summertime in Lockhaven, TX seemed to be long, when in fact it was just a moment's time with anything and everything that could happen.

"Juan, you ready for the day?" Carlisle had two horses at the ready for him and his friend.

"Yes, my friend." Juan appeared to be outfitted for a full day of horseback riding.

"We won't be out for a day." Carlisle snickered at his friend, but not loud enough to hurt his feelings.

"Oh? I thought we go hunt." The slightly smaller man seemed a little depressed.

"I guess we can do a little something." Carlisle reached for his holster and gun, slipping them on.

Juan's countenance changed in a heartbeat and mounted his horse. "We go hunt now?"

Carlisle laughed. "Yes, we'll go now."

The sun rose over the treetops, the two men seemed like long-time best friends. They joked some along the way and shot their guns every once in a while, scaring out anything they could get a shot at. Juan nailed a rabbit so him and his wife could prepare rabbit stew for them and their children.

Carlisle squeezed off a round and scored a buck, out of season though. After a while, the men dismounted their rides and got themselves a drink from a well-watered spring on Carlisle's property. They surveyed the property Carlisle owned and admired God's beauty of having created such a lovely place.

"You own?" Juan mused.

"My dad worked hard for this land." Carlisle offered.

"Lot of land." Juan clapped his hand on Carlisle's shoulder. As they looked around, they soon saw someone crawling out from the bushes on Carlisle's property. They both drew guns and waited.

THREE

"Hey, guys," Beau rasped. He looked like someone had worked him over real well.

"Take it easy, Beau. Be slow."

Carlisle grimaced at his neighbor. "Do you know how you got out here?"

"No, I don't reckon I do." He sobered.

"No tracks." Juan looked to Carlisle.

Carlisle looked both back at the way Juan and him had come as well as any other way, carefully making sure he didn't disturb anything. "Right, Juan. No other tracks leading in or out except us. Do you remember how you got out here, Beau?"

Looking up into his friend and neighbor's face, Beau shook his head. "Nope. Can't say I recall."

"Juan, look him over for me and see if he's okay other than that bump on his head." Carlisle mounted his horse quickly and rode off at a gallop.

I reveled in the moment, knowing Carlisle would be hard-pressed and stumped over who had a hand in this. I laughed silently to myself thinking this was all too easy. First, I got rid of Jakes, being able to acquire his property that was next to Carlisle's. Then I carefully mapped out the terrain of his property to try and dispose of Beau. He, however, was difficult to get rid of. I kept easy pressure on my side, which poured blood as he knifed me good in the belly. I was going to have to lay low for a while.

    Medics came and checked Beau over noting other than the bump on his head everything else was fine.
    "Beau, just in case, go with them to the hospital and if everything is indeed fine, I'll bring you home." Carlisle looked a little worse for wear.
    "What about horses, Carlisle?" Juan held the reins of the horses while looking at his capable friend.
    "Help me load them up into the cargo here, Juan." Carlisle opened the gate to the cargo hold for the horses and they took their time in getting them inside. "Are you boys going to be okay in getting Beau to the hospital?"
    The first medic stood stoically. "Yes, sir. We can get him checked in and all. We'll make sure to get a hold of you when he's ready to be released."
    "All right then, come on Juan. Beau I'll come for you after I get these horses penned up." Carlisle stepped up into his truck cabin.
    At the hospital Carlisle helped Beau get into the truck. "So anything come to mind?"
    Once Carlisle settled in on the driver's side, Beau looked at him oddly. "I wasn't sure if I should say, but some guy with jet-black hair sacked me and dragged me out on to your property."
    Hearing that Carlisle stiffened. "Guy with jet-black hair. How did he sound, Beau?"
    As they drove away from the hospital northward towards Lockhaven Beau saw a raven land close by on wires between electrical poles. "He sounded kind of like a whining bird. Almost like a raven."

A Deadly Game

Carlisle's eyes flashed. It couldn't be! The last time he saw Raven was when Eliza had been shot in the chest and hovered between life and death. His mouth went dry. "Are you sure?"

Beau stole a glance at him. "Positive."

Carlisle's grip on the steering wheel tightened, showing white knuckles.

"Uh, your driving is creeping me out!"

Carlisle loosened his grip a little and got the long hard stare out of his eyes. "Just thought of something is all."

After Beau had been dropped off at his home to be cared for by his wife, Mrs. Olivia Hansen, Carlisle drove over to the Sheriff's office. "Is Hank in?"

Sheril Haines looked up. "No, Carlisle. He isn't. Something I can do you for?" She had a pencil over her right ear, with reading glasses atop her nose, just barely. Her hair was a curly auburn color, which offset her gray eyes. She looked and reminded Carlisle of a schoolteacher.

"I'll stick around a few minutes and see if he shows up." He had his hat in his hands and paced in front of the bay windows of the police station. The police station was a bit antiseptic in its look. The walks were a cream color if at all that, with flooring that was reminiscent of a sterile hospital. On one of the walls hung posters of men wanted by the law. These were hunted men by the officers of Lochaven. Some of them were men Carlisle knew and some weren't. No, Raven's picture was yet to be put up there. He turned away in disgust. The door of the station opened and Hank Oliver ambled in. "Hey, Carlisle. What's up, man?"

"Mind if we talked in your office." He looked grim. Hank Oliver had been Carlisle's former boss from a few years back, before Eliza's murder. He often tried to get Carlisle to come back to work on the force. Yet, he also knew Carlisle was gunning for his job, which elections took place a month from now. "Sure. Does this have to do with Beau, Jakes and Abel?"

Carlisle smiled, knowing his old boss and friend knew him well enough. "Actually, yes."

"You realize I can't bring you back on the force when things are in upheaval, right?"

Carlisle slapped his pant leg with his hat and then let his arm hang there a moment. "I do recognize that. Is there any way I could help out, until things are resolved?"

Hank scratched the right side of his face. He replaced the hat on his head with his arm and looked up at Carlisle. "I can't stop you from being the man that you are. But I can stop you if you try anything related to vigilantism."

Carlisle sighed and sat down across from Hank. "Look, I know you need all the help you can get. It's not like Paul Davison is a swift man. He's a good man and does his job, but he's just not swift."

Hank blew out a low whistle and nodded. "I know that and I appreciate your concern." Hank groped for some kind of an idea. "I know you're after my job, Carlisle. I can't stop you from winning it. Too many people like you and support you. I know I do and I'm tired. I want to be able to retire and soon."

"Then let's stop brow-beating around, Hank. You can deputize me right now if you wanted. Then all you have to do is step down and name me to succeed you." Carlisle stared at the man intently.

Hank sighed yet again, this time thinking the whole exchange between them. "I suppose you want whoever's causing all the damage and killing our residents?"

A Deadly Game

"Yes, sir, I do." Carlisle let his hat drop onto the Sheriff's desk.

Hank stood up first and then had Carlisle do the same. "Do you, Carlisle, swear to uphold the law, to protect the citizens of Lockhaven and surrounding areas, to bring justice and help those in need so help you God?"

"I do." Carlisle looked relieved and so did Hank.

Hank extended his hand across the table to Carlisle, giving him back his old badge. "You're back on the force, Carlisle. Don't blow it."

"Thank you, sir." He picked up his hat and both men started for the door of Hank's office. As they walked into the station lobby and were about to leave the building Carlisle saw movement on top of the feed store. "Duck!"

At the moment that glass shattered with everyone out of the line of fire, Sheril was knocked in her shoulder by a bullet. "Get him! Get him! Whoever and where ever he is!"

Both men got into position and returned shots where the original came from. Someone could be heard laughing in a high-pitched voice and into the night.

"I guess he got what he wanted then." Carlisle stood and surveyed the damage.

While medics tended to the scratch on Sheril's arm, Hank questioned Carlisle. "Okay, so what in blazes is going on?"

"Do you recall the man who killed Eliza?" Carlisle gave his deposition to Hank.

"Yes, vaguely."

"I thought I captured him, but somehow he got free from me and got away." Carlisle sighed and slumped where he stood.

"Don't worry about it, we'll get him. What's his handle?"

"He goes by the name Raven." Carlisle remained standing and watched his boss call all men to the station. In what seemed like just moments the entire force was assembled. "Okay gentlemen, and women, we have a man on the loose by the name of Raven. He is dangerous, cunning and very swift. Should any of you catch the man call either Carlisle or me. We'll take it from there. We can't risk anyone else getting hurt or dying. Dismissed!"

Indeed I got what I wanted, but also at the same time I wanted far more than my old nemesis to be a peace officer again. I wanted to make him suffer. And while yes, my name is Raven as I love those types of birds, my true identity is Stuart LaCasey. Back when Carlisle and I had been friends, once upon a time, he allowed me to take a beating and I held a grudge against him since. Now I follow after him, doing what I can to make him as miserable as he made me feel. One by one I will destroy him and his life if it's the last thing I do!

Carlisle stopped driving a moment, going back to his home, and felt a shiver go up his spine. "Lord, I know I haven't talked to you in ages. I ask for your guidance and protection going into the unknown here. You directed my steps once before and I need you now more than ever. Whatever this guy's beef with me is I ask for your help and for your peace; in the name of Jesus, Amen." He put his truck back into drive and drove onward home.

A Deadly Game

Over the next few weeks everything was put in place for the upcoming election. Most, if not all the votes were in, and they all favored Carlisle becoming Sheriff over Lockhaven. Everyone gathered at the gym of the high school where the announcement became official.

"Ladies and gentlemen." Hank stood proudly. "It is with great honor and pride that I step down as your Sheriff and hand over my badge to your new Sheriff, Carlisle!" The crowd erupted all around Hank. And even though he was stepping down from the position, everyone greeted him and clapped him on the shoulder wishing him well.

Beau walked over to Carlisle, took his hat off and dumped water on him.

"Beau! You shouldn't have done that!"

He still stood grinning though.

Out in the parking lot, where the former Sheriff was getting ready to leave, however, a silhouette dashed from behind the gymnasium and made the kill-shot from fifty feet away. Everyone inside the gym heard the shots and ran outside to see what was going on. Maria was the first to Hank.

"Are you okay, Hank? Hank?"

But there was no pulse. It seemed like everything in Lockhaven was draped in mourning clothes. The sky opened up and rains drenched everything in sight.

"It's a good thing emergency crews are close by." Carlisle grimaced.

Crews and everyone moved to get Hank into the ambulance. They hurried and tried to resuscitate him three times to no avail. The doctor at the Marble Falls Baylor Scott and White pronounced Hank dead at 9:30pm that night.

Slamming the door to his home, Carlisle yelled. "This is now more than personal!" It was also a good thing Amy already left for her parents in Kent, UK. Yet she'd know the truth before she got back to her home with Carlisle. He slammed his hands on the dresser, hard, and just threw everything on top to the floor.

When he realized what he had done, he sat against the opposite wall, allowing himself to both slump and sob openly. While Carlisle wasn't always open to emotional outbursts or even very often, he did so at the loss of which he felt.

"First, my wife, Eliza is taken from me. Next it was Jakes. What did he have to go for? Who did he ever hurt? And while Beau and Sheril weren't hurt badly they didn't deserve to be shot at. And now Hank's dead? What is this guy after? What is warranting his attacks, not just on me and my friends, but on this unsuspecting community?"

He stopped crying, slowly stood up and faced the outside, just from the safety and security of his home.

"Eliza, forgive me, hon. I know I promised to never allow my emotions get the best of me, but I will do all I can to uphold the law and see justice for you, Hank and whoever else before this creep strikes again and hurting anyone else."

FOUR

After some time had passed and Amy returned home to Carlisle, things settled down enough for him to swear in Juan as his deputy. He kept Paul Davison on, allowing him to keep his shift and all he did for the station.

Amy walked into the station where Carlisle sat at his desk. "Here you go, Carlisle. Fresh fruits and a ham sandwich."

Carlisle poked around at what had been offered and inhaled the sandwich as if it were nothing. "Always good, Amy."

"Dang! I never saw anyone just engulf their meal so quickly." He smiled at her as she stood by his desk.

"Sheriff?" Juan walked in motioning for his friend and boss.

"What's going on Juan?" Carlisle uncrossed his legs and got up to stand, walking over to Juan. Juan had been deputized ever since he passed his classes and received citizenship. That was now a month ago. "Paul and I found this piece of burned wood close to your property."

Upon inspecting the burnt out piece of wood it simply said "Cambodia" on it. "What does that mean, boss?"

Carlisle mulled it over and thought back to when Eliza and him had been there to help starving children in the Indonesian area. "Amy, I guess you better hear this as well." He sighed and at back down. "Eliza and I had been there on business, helping children with food and clean water. While we were there she was targeted and killed by an assassin named Raven. I assume he's the same man who gunned down both Hank and Jakes. He's slippery and highly educated. I guess he not only fashions himself an assassin but also as a spy."

Amy drew a deep breath and furrowed her brow in amazement at him. "You mean the man who's been causing grief here is the same one who killed my sister?" Her voice sounded serious and sober.

Carlisle watched her and spoke plainly. "The one and the same."

Amy erupted. "That no good, sister killing goon will deal with…"

"Amy, I won't say this again, but that's my job. Juan and Paul may have to help me out when that time comes, but we'll get him." He looked bound as he spoke to her.

"It better be soon, or I'll be the one putting a bullet in him." She swore.

"Miss Amy, too many people died. I don't want anything happening to you." Juan looked apologetically at her.

"He's right, Amy. We'll get him when the time comes, in the meantime why don't you go home and rest?"

Carlisle waited for any news from their monitoring unit. Nothing came over the airwaves. All was quiet at the moment except for static.

"Fine, but if I ever have the chance I'll fill him with shot if I have to." She left angrily, stomping

A Deadly Game

out of the station.

"What was that about?" Paul walked in as Amy climbed into her car and drove towards their home.

"Oh, she's just a little hot under the collar about things. She'll be fine. What have you got for me, Paul?"

Paul stared in the same direction, mouth hanging open at how Amy left.

"Not much, sir. Stopped a break in and that's why Clyde's in a holding cell."

Carlisle poked his head around to the holding cells. "Clyde, you up?"

"Howdy, Sheriff." Clyde shuffled about in his cell.

"What on earth possessed you to..."

He looked over the report. "To steal pigs?"

"I thought them pigs was after me." He stood solemnly.

"Well, Clyde, that's a sorry excuse for pig-theft. I'm afraid you'll have to stay another night until we get a judge to listen to the charges."

Clyde spat on the floor. "You no good...!"

"Now, Clyde, you might sit yourself on down and cool off before I have to come in there and deal with you." Carlisle brewed like a teakettle close to finishing up.

Clyde took a breath and let it loose slowly, sitting down on the bunk
in the holding cell.

Once Carlisle's shift was over and Shawn covered the evening shift, he went on home to Amy. Nothing real spectacular happened on the drive home, he just noticed storm clouds brewing overhead and turned the lights on as he drove home. "It looks like it might be a wild night, storm-wise."

As he got out of his truck and sauntered into his house, Amy burst out of the kitchen startling him.

"Amy, you could plum scare a chicken if nothing else was happening!"

She took one look at Carlisle, helped him up. "I am so, so sorry. I didn't mean to, I was just happy you got home safely." She gave him a kiss on the cheek, something she rarely did. "So, what would you think if we settled down, Carlisle?"

He set his holster on the right side of the back of his chair, took his hat off and beheld her gaze with his. He drew a deep breath. "Amy, I'm really flattered and all..."

"If you keep putting things off with me, I may just leave and go home to Kent." She pouted.

"Look, Amy, it's complicated." He tried hugging her.

"Look nothing." Thunder rolled outside as raindrops started pounding the rooftop.

"Let me phrase it better, then." He wilted some.

"Yes?" She eyeballed him out of curiosity.

He exhaled and thought for a moment. "Alright, I wanted to wait until things were settled but since you can't seem to be patient." He pulled a box out of his pocket and got down on one knee. "Amy Moore, would you do me the honor of being my wife?"

She exploded into sobs, wrapping her arms around him and pulling him up. "Yes! Oh, God, yes, I will be your wife!"

He wondered how the night had gone had he not proposed. While he hated the thought of her ever leaving him, he simply couldn't be without a memory of Eliza either. He just kept praying and hoping she would never know this.

A Deadly Game

Lovebirds, so disgusting it makes me literally sick. I sat on the edge of a rooftop next door to their home watching them hug. I was so glad to be enshrouded in darkness. I wanted so badly to just put an end to this all, but I knew if I did anything, at this moment or even soon would just send him into a homicidal mess against me. No, the smart thing to do was just wait my time. I had to wait things out and prolong things. In the end it would make perfect sense. In the end he'd know why I killed his first wife. So I left them to be in their sickness called happiness.

When the sun rose, all traces of the rain the night before disappeared. Sure the grass looked happy and healthy, but other than that everything looked dry. By the time the day ended it would be back to hot and dry with no rain in sight for the next ten or so days.
"Sam!?" Carlisle entered his favorite place to eat breakfast.
"Why, Carlisle, it's been so long I wondered what was keeping you away!"
The two friends hugged each other quickly and Sam went after a cup of coffee for Carlisle. "So, Amy liked the ring?" He chuckled.
Carlisle was shocked momentarily with the coffee inches from his mouth. "How'd you know?"
"Don't burn yourself, now. She breezed in just fifteen minutes before you, showing off that really nice and lovely ring." He bemused at Carlisle.
Sam was a man's man, but at times could be a true softy when it came to his patrons having either a good day or when love was in the air. He was slightly balding at his forehead, appearing a little rotund for his frame but otherwise seemed like a Santa Claus type overall.

Carlisle considered this a moment and drank his coffee. "So, did she say anything as to where she was headed, Sam?"

Sam welcomed two new guests into his establishment and returned to the topic at hand. "Yes, she was going over to Suller's Creek, she said."

"Thanks, Sam." Carlisle got up, paid for his coffee and headed out that way to the Creek.

It took only a few minutes from the coffee shop to the creek and sure enough there was Amy's car. Her car was easily identifiable to Carlisle. It was a light blue hatchback, four door Kia Rio. He also had the license plate memorized. No one drove one around in Lockhaven, no one except for her.

"Amy?" He looked for her.

She stood up and looked his way. "Hey, right here."

Carlisle walked over to where she was and sat down next to her. "I got your letter telling me we were picnicking, but you forgot where to say where to come."

She laughed in her own fun way. "But you figured it out with Sam's help."

He looked into her eyes and regarded her. "Which is true, but you could at least say so I don't feel I'm on a treasure hunt."

Just as they were about to have lunch in the open air of Suller's Creek and have a nice, lazy day of enjoying each other a scream tore at the seams. "Stay here with the food, Amy." He warned.

She grabbed his arm. "No, way. I'm coming with."

"If you do, just be careful. There's no way I want two lives on the line." He watched her as they moved forward into Suller's Creek proper. They heard more screams as they drew close unknowing what they'd find.

Carlisle wished inside of himself he knew for sure what was happening as they climbed a small ridge, but had Amy duck so nothing would happen to her. As they cleared the top, they looked down and saw happy bodies jumping from a cliff into the creek below. Both of them drew a breath and let it out slowly, having thought something was wrong.

"I guess we've both been on edge lately, huh?" Amy looked to her man.

"I suppose so, Amy. What's with that look?" He noticed her getting ready to pounce him.

She poised herself over him and jumped at the hooded figure, fingernails bared.

She came down on me and hard. I had no time to shoot at Carlisle and she tore my flesh. Had I been any quicker and he'd be dead, lying in his own blood. But it just wasn't my day. I thought I camped out well enough and in the right spot to get him and then be able to pop her just for good measure. Then I felt his hands grapple me down, pinning me to the ground. I snarled and snapped as he handcuffed me, like a turtle does when handled wrong.

"Okay, Raven. Now, tell me your rightful name?" Carlisle fumed.

"Stuart LaCasey!" The man with gothic paint on his face screamed out. The partygoers who were once having fun stopped and stared in their direction.

"There's nothing to see here folks, just go about your own business and have fun in the creek. Just be careful where you swim is all." Carlisle dragged Stuart, the Raven, all the way back to his truck, cuffing him to the side.

"Carlisle?" Amy stood there panting as Carlisle finished up by reading Stuart his rights.

"What is it, Amy?" Carlisle turned and noticed she was scared, shaking. He closed the passenger side of his truck door and walked over to her. "You okay?"

She wrapped her arms around him and buried her head into his chest. "I am now. I'm glad you finally got him, Carlisle. We, I mean. Now Eliza can rest in peace."

After it had been revealed through a trial as to why Stuart LaCasey killed first Eliza Moore as well as Hank Oliver no arraignment for his release was needed. Both sides agreed Stuart needed jail time to think through his actions to all involved. Stuart had once been in love with and dated Eliza.

When he lost her due to her marrying Carlisle he sought after vengeance. Stuart claimed under oath, "Hank was just the icing on the cake."

And if it had not been for the bailiff and other officers of the law Carlisle would have hurt him then and there. Now that Stuart was on his way to State Penitentiary for committing two first degree murders the town of Lockhaven was ready to be normal once more.

The day Amy and Carlisle were wed the town turned out for the affair. Both were united and called as "man and wife," where afterward he kissed his bride and they honeymooned in Bora Bora. Nothing could be happier for the newly married Donovan's and the town of Lockhaven, TX. No more terror would visit it again.

A Deadly Game

If only this place where I sit now knew how much I have dug within this last week into the wall, they'd hook me up and give me the death penalty. I just kept on grinning.

ABOUT BENJAMIN LILES

Benjamin H. Liles has previously written *The Prodigal Son* as a self-published book. This is his second book to date, and he lives in the Texas Hill Country with his wife and two cats.

Made in the USA
Coppell, TX
19 February 2026

71799130R00022